and the
# SEASIDE SOS

For Maisie
J.S.

For Dana Mae
C.E.

Reading Consultant: Prue Goodwin, Lecturer in literacy and children's books

ORCHARD BOOKS
338 Euston Road, London NW1 3BH
*Orchard Books Australia*
Level 17/207 Kent Street, Sydney, NSW 2000

First published in 2012
First paperback publication in 2013

ISBN 978 1 40831 331 2 (hardback)
ISBN 978 1 40831 339 8 (paperback)

A CIP catalogue record for this book is available from the British Library.

1 3 5 7 9 10 8 6 4 2 (hardback)
1 3 5 7 9 10 8 6 4 2 (paperback)

Printed in China

Orchard Books is a division of Hachette Children's Books,
an Hachette UK company.

and the
# SEASIDE SOS

## Justine Smith • Clare Elsom

ORCHARD

Zak Zoo lives at Number One, Africa Avenue.
His mum and dad are away on
safari, so his animal family is looking
after him. Sometimes things get a little . . .

. . . WILD!

Dad

Mum

Tom

Pam

Zak

Nanny
Hilda

Rosa
and
Rupert

Boris

Verity and
Violet

Max

Mia (Zak's best friend)

It was Saturday morning, and Zak had just written a letter to his mum and dad. He gave it to the post-bird, Tom.

Tom flew off to deliver the letter.

Dear Mum and Dad,

I hope you are well.
Today we are going to the
beach.

Love, Zak

Zak and his animal family lined up to get on the bus to the beach. But the driver looked worried. So did Zak's friend, Mia.

"This will be fun!" said Zak.

Rupert sat at the back of the bus and broke the seat.

Verity and Violet sat on the roof and made a dent.

Max sat on the bonnet and snapped the windscreen wipers.

The driver was cross about the damage to his bus. Then he saw Zak eating some crisps.

"No food allowed on my bus!" the driver said.

At last they were on their way.

Everyone was excited about going to the beach.

"What about a song?" said Zak.

"No singing on my bus!" said the

bus driver.

Everyone stopped singing. But the bus started making funny noises. There was a *hisss* and a *psss*, and then a long *sssss*.

"That sounds like a puncture," said Zak.

The driver stopped the bus.

Everyone got off, feeling sad.

Would they ever get to the beach?

"Can we help?" said Zak.

Rupert lifted up the bus while the driver changed the wheel.

Everyone got back on the bus
feeling much happier!

17

They drove along again quite happily until Max got bored and broke the sat nav. Then Boris ate the emergency map.

"I know!" said Zak. "Verity and Violet can show us the way!"
The vultures flew towards the sea.

Finally, Zak and his animal
family arrived at the beach.
It was a lovely, sunny day and
some of them went for a swim.
Everyone else got out of the water.

"Stay and play!" said Pam.
But everyone ran away except for the
bus driver. He rolled up his trousers
and started eating an ice cream.

Zak sat in a deck chair and wrote his mum and dad a postcard.

Dear Mum and Dad,

We are having a rest at the beach. It's very quiet here.

Love,
Zak

As Zak stuck a stamp on his postcard, there was a sudden flash, far out to sea.

"What's that?" said Mia.

Zak looked through his binoculars
and saw a boat sinking. He called
his animal family over to help.

Mia brought some lifejackets.

"All the good swimmers, go and save those people!" said Zak. Zak's animal family swam out to the sinking boat while he shouted directions from the shore.

Soon the people from the boat
were safe back on the beach.
"Thank you!" they said.

The bus driver was impressed too.

"Good work!" he told Zak.

Zak and his animal family climbed

back onto the bus.

"What about a song?" said the driver.

And they sang all the way home.

Written by *Justine Smith* • Illustrated by *Clare Elsom*

Zak Zoo and the School Hullabaloo    978 1 40831 329 9

Zak Zoo and the Peculiar Parcel    978 1 40831 330 5

Zak Zoo and the Seaside SOS    978 1 40831 331 2

Zak Zoo and the Unusual Yak    978 1 40831 332 9

Zak Zoo and the Hectic House    978 1 40831 333 6

Zak Zoo and the Baffled Burglar    978 1 40831 334 3

Zak Zoo and the TV Crew    978 1 40831 335 0

Zak Zoo and the Birthday Bang    978 1 40831 336 7

All priced at £8.99

Orchard Books are available from all good bookshops,
or can be ordered from our website: www.orchardbooks.co.uk,
or telephone 01235 827702, or fax 01235 827703.

Prices and availability are subject to change.